I0691004

**Berty Ashley** is a molecular biologist with the Dystrophy Annihilation Research Trust and works with rare genetic disorders. What is not rare though is to see him conducting quizzes or attending them. He is the author of the popular *Easy Like Sunday Morning* series of quizzes published in *The Hindu Sunday* magazine. Berty is also a lover of music—not only playing but collecting, as is evident by his growing stack of vinyl records of Jazz, Prog, Hindustani and Heavy metal music. He and his partner, Akhila, live in Bengaluru, surrounded by books, music, and an assortment of pens and guitars.

**Akhila Phadnis** is a freelance translator. She holds a Masters in Translation Studies from Durham University, UK, and in Psychology from Madras University, Chennai, Tamil Nadu. She enjoys reading, practicing calligraphy, learning new languages, quizzing, board games, and taking long walks by the beach.

# The MIGHTY QUIZ

## BERTY ASHLEY
### AND
## AKHILA PHADNIS

RUPA

Published by
Rupa Publications India Pvt. Ltd 2019
7/16, Ansari Road, Daryaganj
New Delhi 110002

*Sales centres:*
Allahabad Bengaluru Chennai
Hyderabad Jaipur Kathmandu
Kolkata Mumbai

ISBN: 978-93-5333-598-4

First impression 2019

10 9 8 7 6 5 4 3 2 1

# INTRODUCTION

'General Knowledge', or GK, as we have all heard about in school is usually defined as 'culturally valued knowledge encompassing a wide subject range'. Sometimes GK may just seem to be a subject needed to pass certain sections in entrance examinations. However, over time, all of us realize that this GK helps in various other aspects of life as well. Having some sort of GK leads to informed civil discourse and opinions that tend to shape a person's life. As *Forbes* Magazine pointed out, 'without a common core of general knowledge, how can one ascertain the historical significance of an event, let alone if the event ever existed? Ditto for geography or world-historical figures, whether good, bad or ugly'. The CoreKnowledge Foundation says that 'Research consistently shows that strong readers have a substantial store of background knowledge that helps them make connections as they read and make correct inferences about things they don't know. The more you know, the easier it is for you to understand what you read and to learn new things.'

What the authors can tell you from experience is that maintaining a wide breadth of GK will not only help you academically but can be very useful in everyday conversation, networking, job interviews, dating and public speaking. It could be said that the pros and cons of GK are the same thing—the absolute vastness and infinite amount of information there is. The pro is that you will always find something new; the con is that you will never be able to satisfactorily know everything in any field and may spend your life constantly looking for new information. This is precisely why the authors of this book have decided to skip dividing the information into specific chapters of any kind in this book!

All the questions in this book have been broadly classified into three sections: questions that have a 'What?', 'Where?' and 'Who?'. These three simple words encompass mankind's eternal quest for knowledge. The questions 'Which?', 'How?', 'Why? and 'When?' have been integrated into these three as well. We don't claim to be experts, neither do we postulate that the information we have here is the absolute essence of all information and knowledge in the world. What we have put together in this book are simply facts and trivia that we have come across in our lives, which have stunned or awed us and that we love sharing with people. These have been presented to you in such a way as to incite interest and, if a new fact, hopefully make you go, 'That was so cool! I had no idea!'

One of the interesting issues posed by this decision to cover as many subjects as possible without dividing them into chapters was how to present the questions. We took the easy way out and decided to offer to the reader sets of 10 questions, with various themes jumbled together. We hope this will keep you engrossed and also allow you to take your time and explore the book at your own pace, flipping back and forth. There is no order, so mix and match the questions as you will!

We hope you have as much fun solving these questions as we did setting them. We have tried to avoid including any time-bound facts, which might not hold good if you were to read this book say, 5 years from now (such as records, which may be broken within a month of this book being published!). But since the world is full of staggering impossibilities, we would love to hear from readers at any point in the future that one of these records or numbers change! The same holds true for all information in the book—we have taken great care to verify and find strong, reliable evidence, but we are always open to discussing our references with any inquisitive reader. Ultimately, all we want is for you to have a good read every time you pick up this book. Happy quizzing!

**What?**

# SET I

1. In 1945, Percy Spencer was working near high-powered vacuum tubes used in radar equipment when he realized that a candy bar in his pocket had melted. This led him to bring different objects near the equipment, including an egg that reportedly exploded in the face of an engineer who peeped over to get a look at it. Spencer saw the potential in this accidental discovery and along with his employers, Raytheon, patented a device that was sold, in 2 years, as the first commercial microwave oven. Given the company's specialization until then, under what name was this first model sold?

2. To continue from the above question—Spencer wanted to test this device and brought various foods into the lab to check how they cooked or reacted to the 'microwaves'. According to most reports, what was the first food item he deliberately tested, which is something that a lot of people use microwave ovens for today?

3. This sportsperson, rather interestingly, is named after

a legendary sportsperson in her field. Her mother and coach, Melanie Molitor, wanted to name her daughter after the sporting legend from their country, the erstwhile Czechoslovakia, hoping her daughter would follow a similar career trajectory. The person she is named after is arguably the greatest player in her sport, with 59 major titles and over 300 career titles. She is also an openly gay player and activist. The younger sportsperson went on to win 5 major singles titles, 13 doubles titles and 7 mixed doubles titles (a total of 25 Grand Slam titles!), also becoming the youngest ever player to win Wimbledon, when she won the doubles, the youngest player since the 1880s at the Australian Open, and also the youngest player to become world number one. While the older namesake left Czechoslovakia to become an American citizen (re-applying for Czech nationality as a second nationality in 2008), the younger player became a Swiss citizen after her mother moved to Switzerland. What name do these two greats share?

4. When the famous explorer Robert Scott wrote back from his final polar expedition, he mentioned the supplies he was carrying. This included Oxo, a British brand of _____. Oxo saw this as the perfect advertising opportunity and put out an advertisement showing certain animals lining up to dip into a pot of Oxo. However, fortunately they were warned that their depictions were wrong and they were able to replace these with another set of animals, resulting in a very cute advertisement. What was the first

animal they had portrayed and why did they remove them?

5. During Robert Scott's final polar expedition, he had travelled with a team of scientists and they had set out with several clear goals in mind. One of these was to try and establish a certain geological fact that scientists had long speculated about. When the remains of Scott's team were discovered, certain important fossils were discovered among their possessions. These fossils were the same as others discovered in Australia, Africa and South America and thus proved the scientists' theory regarding a geological feature as well as a climate-related theory. What were these two theories?

6. In addition to penguin eggs, Robert Scott's final polar expedition had also collected penguin skins. These skins, which were collected in 1912, proved to be crucial evidence around 50 years later, to show that a certain chemical had reached the Antarctic. The skins essentially showed the complete absence of a certain chemical that was found in penguins 50 years later. What is this chemical that has now reached the ends of the earth and which played a huge role in agriculture for many years, before being banned for its environmental impact?

7. Conscious of the power of the relatively new technology of photography, Robert Scott took along an official photographer on his final polar expedition, to document the incredibly new regions they were exploring. Herbert Ponting, the photographer, took many photos and

managed to film some interesting behaviour. Among these was the behaviour of a pack of whales that Ponting was keen on filming. What he did not realize, however, was that the whales would also be interested in him! He felt the ice heaving under him as the whales made coordinated movements to beat the water with their tails so that large waves would knock him off the ice and into the sea. What is this movement or strategy used by the whales now known as?

8. In conditions of excess heat or exertion in heat, a person may suffer from a heatstroke, during which their body temperature soars and the internal tissue and organs may be damaged. Because the body is getting dehydrated, it conserves water and redirects fluid around internal organs to try and cool them. This produces one of the characteristic symptoms of heatstroke, where the body stops performing a very natural function that is usually associated with higher temperatures. What is this vital function that otherwise helps to cool the body?

9. In the 1860s, there was a naval battle between a Uruguayan ship and a Brazilian one. The Uruguayans ran out of ammunition at one point and their commander, Captain Coe, recalled something else they had on board. He ordered his men to load this into the cannons and fire it at the enemy. One of these missiles actually reached its target and shattered the mast of the ship, also killing some sailors standing nearby. When more missiles were fired at their sails, the Brazilians finally withdrew. What

was the strange missile that Captain Coe had used?

10. Anuradha Pal is the first soloist on a certain instrument that is dominated by male musicians in India. She learnt this instrument when her brother was being taught and while his teacher initially refused to teach her, when she taught herself and played for him he was very impressed and agreed to take her on as a student. She counts among her gurus, two of the world's greatest musicians who play this instrument and has herself gone on to earn accolades for her virtuosity and work as a composer. In 1996, she set up the all-female band Stree Shakti to promote women musicians in India. What is Anuradha Pal's instrument of choice?

## ANSWERS

1. Rada Range
2. Popping corn kernels (the first microwave popcorn)
3. Martina (Martina Hingis was named after Martina Navratilova)
4. Polar bears. Scott's expedition was to the South Pole and there are no polar bears at the South Pole, thus the final advertisement used penguins
5. The existence of a supercontinent and the fact that the Antarctic once had a mild climate allowing trees and other vegetation to flourish
6. DDT: Dichlorodiphenyltrichloroethane

7. Wave-washing
8. Sweating
9. Stale cheeses
10. Tabla. She is the first woman table soloist

# SET 2

11. In 2018, the Supreme Court of India struck down one of India's most discriminatory laws, a remnant of the colonial era. Although this law had already been struck down in 2009, the Supreme Court had overturned this decision in 2013 stating that this legislation should happen through parliament, rather than through the courts. Activists had moved court, stating that this was an unconstitutional law and that governments were not taking this up in parliament. In a historic judgement that quoted from Leonard Cohen, Vikram Seth and William Shakespeare (among others!) this law was struck down. What was this law and what normal human behaviour had it criminalized?

12. In 1973, citizens of the Polish town of Bydgoszcz woke up to find that their drinking water taps were supplying them with beer instead! Before they could get used to this new state of things, the explanation was found and the problem was fixed. What had caused this interesting phenomenon?

13. This phenomenon has been dubbed a certain rule and states that in any online community, there is only a certain percentage of members that actively engages and creates new content, while a much larger percentage 'lurks'. A number between these two groups reacts or responds to the new content created, but does not actively create content of its own. What is the name by which this phenomenon is generally known, which may describe most group projects?

14. If you are visiting Scotland, it would be wise to refuse a 'Glasgow kiss'. What would you get if you accepted?

15. Marketing genius Charles Foster noticed young boys selling _____ made of Spanish willow on his trip to Brazil. He returned to Boston in 1870 and set up a mass production factory to produce this item using birch as a material, because it was tasteless. What business did Foster thus begin?

16. Ariadne was the daughter of Minos, king of Crete. Her father put her in charge of the labyrinth where sacrifices were made as part of reparations to Athena. This maze was guarded by a creature called a Minotaur, with the head of a bull on the body of a man. Ariadne helped her lover Theseus overcome the Minotaur by using a ball of thread to help him out of the maze. Which word in the English language is derived from that ball of thread?

17. This animal has killed the most number of people in history. They kill more than 700,000 people every year and are estimated to have killed more than 5 billion

people over the course of human civilization. Which animal is this?

18. In 1949, a young entrepreneur, K. M. Mammen Mappillai, opened a small toy balloon manufacturing unit in a shed at Tiruvottiyur, Madras (now Chennai). Although the factory was just a small shed without any machines, a variety of products, ranging from balloons and squeaking toys to industrial gloves and contraceptives, were produced. Which multi-billion-dollar company had such a humble beginning?

19. Götterdämmerung (Twilight of the Gods) is the last one in Richard Wagner's cycle of four music dramas, called 'The Ring', which runs for 15 hours. The title is a translation of the Old Norse word 'Ragnarök' into German. In Norse mythology, this word refers to a prophesied war among various beings and gods that ultimately results in the burning, immersion in water and renewal of the world. Valkyrie Brünnhilde, who is traditionally presented as a very fit lady with a horned helmet, spear and round shield, performs an aria that lasts almost twenty minutes and leads directly to the end of the opera. This final sequence of the opera, performed by this character, has given birth to a very famous phrase. What is this phrase?

20. Sir Andre Konstantin Geim is a Soviet-born Dutch-British physicist who discovered a simple method for isolating single atomic layers of graphite, known as graphene. Geim also discovered diamagnetic levitation of water,

using which he levitated a frog. What did these warrant him to become the only one in the world to have?

## ANSWERS

11. Section 377 of the IPC, homosexuality
12. A valve in a brewery had been damaged, resulting in beer flooding into the drinking water pipes in the city
13. The 1 per cent rule
14. A headbutt
15. Toothpicks
16. Clue, from 'Klew'
17. Mosquitoes
18. MRF
19. 'It is only over when the Fat Lady sings.'
20. Only person to have won a Nobel Prize and its spoof counterpart the IgNobel Prize

# SET 3

21. After a certain band finished a concert in Birmingham, the crowd kept clapping and chanting, 'You'll never walk alone'. Based on this emotional experience, the band wrote a song, which was released in 1977, in the album *News of the World*. A delay was used to produce the effect of many people taking part. The durations of the delays were in ratios of prime numbers, a technique now known as non-harmonic reverberation. The credits simply say 'vocals, electric guitar, handclaps, footstomps'. This is the story behind which famous song by which band?

22. This is a new type of ice cream that gets a lot of coverage on Instagram. After unicorns, glitter and sprinkles, this is had by those who crave a dessert that speaks to their inner darkness. This ice cream is named after a member of a Germanic people that overran the Roman Empire. The word also refers to people who are morbid, dressing in black clothes almost all the time and wearing makeup regardless of sex. What is this ice cream called?

23. One of the first palaeontologists in England was a woman named Mary Anning. Along with her brother, she collected a lot of shells and fossils such as ammonites and belemnites from coastal regions in and around her hometown. The two of them made fossils a family business. Her work is said to have contributed to big changes in the way nineteenth-century geologists thought about the history of the earth. Most of us have heard of a rather twisted reference to her created by a P.J. McCartney in his book *Henry de la Benche*. What is the reference?

24. This myth was started by Italian _____makers. They had discovered that sheep intestines were the best for a particular product that they produced. Killing a particular animal was supposed to bring bad luck, so they spread a rumour that their new invention was made from the intestines of these other animals instead of sheep. Today, the gut is mixed with nylon and steel but purists swear that the original is the best. What did the rumour-mongers make and what animal did they make the rumour about?

25. What was the first man-made object to break the sound barrier?

26. According to some, a type of bread was invented in Vienna in 1683, to celebrate the failure of the Turkish army that tried to conquer the city. Legend has it that the Turks dug a tunnel under the walls of Vienna. As the tunnel surfaced in a bakery, the bakers alerted the

citizens and prevented the Turkish soldiers from entering the city. So, a type of bread was created to somehow symbolize this victory. What is the name of this type of bread?

27. These motivational posters were initially intended to be part of a series of three, to boost citizen morale during the Second World War. The first two say, 'Freedom is in Peril. Defend it with All your Might' and 'Your Courage, your Cheerfulness, your Resolution will Bring us Victory'. The third and most famous one was actually largely forgotten at the time and shot to fame when a copy was discovered at a place now called 'Barter Books' in Alnwick. The words on this one have now gained mass popularity and been repeatedly used across the last decade. What are the words?

28. When early American distillers shipped a barrel of whisky, they burnt their signature on one end of the keg. What term did this practice give rise to?

29. This frequently-used application is one of the prime examples of crowdsourcing and is instrumental in negotiating connectivity in the daily lives of many people around the world. The colour coding of this application is its most important feature and is determined as follows: red if it is 25 miles per hour or less, yellow if it is between 25 to 50 miles per hour, blue if it is 50 miles per hour or more. What is being referred to here?

# ANSWERS

21. 'We Will Rock You' by Queen
22. Goth ice cream
23. She sells sea shells on the sea shore
24. Violin string-makers spread the rumour that they made strings from cat gut
25. A whip. The sharp sound made by a whip is the ultrasonic boom caused when the tip of the whip travels faster than the speed of sound
26. Croissant
27. Keep Calm and Carry on
28. Branding
29. Google Maps

# SET 4

30. This spherical confectionary was introduced in 1982 by the company that makes Tic Tac and Nutella, amongst others. The first part of this confectionary's name is the name of the company that manufactures it, and the second part comes from the French word for 'rock'. This confectionary is traditionally associated with Christmas and New Year and in some countries the policy is to market it only during winter. Which confectionary are we talking about?

31. Satoshi Tajiri grew up in Machida, Tokyo. As a boy, he had a habit of collecting bugs and insects in and around his house. He wanted to be an entomologist and his classmates used to call him 'Mr Bug'. As he grew up, his interests changed and he got into what every other Japanese teenager did—gaming. He spent his high school days trying to make his own game. In 1996, he created a game, based on his childhood interests, which took the market by storm. In 2017, with amazing advancements

in technology, what form was the game revived in?

32. Indian tabla player Sandeep Das is a part of Yo-Yo Ma's Ensemble, which has won the Grammy in the World Music category. This ensemble consists of artists from different parts of the globe. The name of their ensemble comes from an ancient network of trade routes that were essential for cultural interaction over centuries. It stretched across Asia to parts of Africa and Europe, connecting the East and West. The route gets its name from the most precious commodity that was traded on this route. What is the name of this ensemble?

33. In this song from a film, the lead actor and actress visit multiple famous monuments: the Great Wall of China, the Eiffel Tower, the Empire State Building, the Taj Mahal, the Pyramids and the Sphinx, the Colosseum and the Leaning Tower of Pisa. This was the most expensive Indian film made at the time of its release and its title was a pun on the fact that the film's lead actor portrayed a pair of identical twins. What is the name of this 1998 Tamil film which was also released in Hindi?

34. There is a certain American eatery chain renowned for staying open through various catastrophic or extreme events. It once stayed open during a devastating tornado! In 2004, the then director of the Federal Emergency Management Agency came up with an index to measure how bad a weather event was, by checking whether or not this chain stayed open. He explained that if a _____ _____ is closed because of disaster, then the conditions

are bad and this disaster is classified as red. If it remains open but has a limited menu, then the classification is yellow. And if it remains open and fully functional, then the classification is green. What is the name of this index, taken directly from the name of the chain?

35. There is a certain method to see if this specific item is good or bad. When these items get old, the gases inside them escape and they absorb air over time through a semi-permeable membrane and form an air bubble. Fresh items do not have that air bubble as they are tightly packed. What items are these and how do you perform this test?

36. Achraszapota is fruit plant we all know. It is grown for the fruit and gum-like substance obtained from latex and is mainly used for preparation of chewing gum. The name of the main compound required to make chewing gum comes from the local name of this fruit. The most popular chewing gum is also named after this compound. What is the name of this fruit?

37. Superbugs are resistant to all antibiotics and are a huge threat to medicine. One mechanism that contributes to antibiotic resistance involves an enzyme called NDM-1. This is responsible for resistance to Klebsiella pneumoniae. NDM-1 was first observed in a Swedish man who fell sick after visiting a certain country. Though it was later seen in other places, the name stuck. M-1 stands for 'Metallobetalactamase-1'. ND stands for a place that

is also referenced in a 2011 cult film. What does ND stand for?

38. Which is the only planet in the Solar System not named after a Roman god? Which star, the nearest star from the earth, is not named after a Roman god?

39. The Sahitya Akademi Award is one of highest literary awards in India. First awarded in 1955 in certain Indian languages, it was not awarded to an English work till 1960, when it went to a certain novel that was also turned into a path-breaking film in 1965. Who is the recipient of the first Sahitya Akademi Award for English and what is the title of their novel?

40. According to food historians, until the fifteenth century, chillies were not used in India and pepper was used instead. Pepper was referred to as in Tamil. So, when vegetables were prepared, the dish was called 'kaai'. For meat preparations, extra _____was used to make the dish spicy. As time passed, the word came to be used differently across the social spectrum, with most using the word to just refer to meat, since that was the dominant ingredient used in meat dishes. In general Tamil parlance, the word means 'meat'. In vegetarian households, it could just mean 'vegetables'. In the West, a modified version of this word is used to refer to a variety of Indian dishes. What is this now-prevalent term?

# ANSWERS

30. Ferrero Rocher
31. Pokémon Go
32. Silk Route
33. Jeans
34. Waffle House
35. Checking eggs by putting them in water
36. Chikoo (which is what chiclets are named after)
37. New Delhi (Delhi Belly)
38. Earth, Sun
39. R.K. Narayanan, *The Guide*
41. Curry, kari

# SET 5

41. After immigrating to the United States from England in 1869, William _____ settled in Racine. In 1872, he went to Chicago to begin a food manufacturing business with his brother James, who had earlier worked in a company that produced powdered baby food from malt and bran. At home, they experimented with wheat and malted barley, which could be stored for long periods in sealed containers. This led to a product called 'Diastoid', which was eventually changed to the surname of the brothers. What is the name of this product which people usually buy when going to visit someone in hospital?

42. This company was founded in 1996 by American entrepreneurs Brewster Kahle and Bruce Gilliat. The company's name was chosen to pay homage to the Library of Alexandria of Ptolemaic Egypt, drawing a parallel between the largest repository of knowledge in the ancient world and the potential of the Internet to become a similar store of knowledge. In 1998, the

company donated a copy of the archive, two terabytes in size, to the Library of Congress. When the parent company introduced a virtual assistant, they chose this name to refer to it. What are the names of the parent company and the assistant?

43. This is a co-operative organization involved in manufacturing a particular edible product. Started in the year 1959 with a seed capital of ₹80, it now has an annual turnover of around ₹6.5 billion (over $100 million) in 2010, with ₹290 million in exports. It provides employment to around 42,000 people. The organization was started by 7 Gujarati women to create a sustainable livelihood using the only skills they had. What path-breaking organization is this?

44. Mozambique's flag has multicoloured stripes and a yellow star. The green stands for the riches of the land, the white lines signify peace, black represents the African continent, yellow symbolizes the country's minerals, and red represents their struggle for independence. There are three items on the star as well: a hoe that represents agriculture and an open book that represents education. The third item makes this flag unique, as it is the only one in the world to have a pictorial representation of this modern weapon. What interesting item is found on the flag of Mozambique, to signify defence and vigilance?

45. *The Onion* is an American satirical newspaper. In recent years, it has used a standard headline to refer to a certain occurrence, stating,

'"No Way To Prevent This," Says Only Nation Where This Regularly Happens.' What tragic event does this headline refer to, sadly too often?

46. This object was initially invented by Walter Hunt to settle a debt of $15 with his friend. It was patented and sold to W.R. Grace and Company for $400, with which amount Mr Hunt settled his debt. The company went on to make millions of dollars out of this product. The object contained a brass wire that was about 8-inches long, with a coil in its centre, so that it would open up when released. The clasp at one end was devised in order to shield the sharp edge from the user. What is this simple object that Hunt invented in 1849?

47. In 1895, in a town named Llanelli in Wales, two brothers, Walter and Tom Davies, opened an ironmongers store on _____Street. They also sold bicycles and later, a motor car business developed there. In 1905, they came up with a revolutionary concept for a car accessory that is still an essential part of cars. The patent/invention was named after the street from which they had started their store. Even today in India, this accessory is referred to by the name of that street in Wales. In Tamil, the word can also be used in local slang as an insult, to refer to someone who is not the main point of interest but a back-up plan. What is this invention and what is its name?

48. In 1940, Alfred Hitchcock made a film based on a Daphne du Maurier classic, starring Laurence Olivier, Joan Fontaine and Judith Anderson. This was Hitchcock's

first American film and was made for David O. Selznick. The producer was shocked at Hitchcock's initial work on the film, stating, 'We bought _____ and we intend to make _____.' What are the names of the film and the book it is based on?

49. In the same film as the previous question, Hitchcock and Selznick also did not see eye to eye on the ending. Selznick apparently wanted a dramatic scene, using smoke from a burning building, while Hitchcock preferred to end with flames consuming an embroidered letter R on a pillowcase. In this instance, Hitchcock's vision prevailed. What was Selznick's far more dramatic idea?

50. In June 2016, a certain referendum was held to determine whether or not a certain country would remain part of a larger body. While politicians in the country had been fairly certain that things would continue as they had been, everyone received a jolt when a slender majority voted to no longer be a part of the larger body. While (as of 2019) the country is still struggling to organize the outcome of this, a certain article in the treaty with the larger body has been triggered. What is the number of this article and what is the name by which this referendum is now being referred to even in the country's parliament, a play on the name of the country and the action it voted for?

51. This response is usually thought to be a camouflage function, based on this animal's surroundings. However, various studies have shown that in reality this characteristic change is driven by moods and emotions!

What animal is this and what is the change associated with it?

## ANSWERS

41. Horlicks
41. Amazon, Alexa
43. Lijjat Papad
44. An AK-47 rifle
45. Mass shootings in the United States of America
46. The safety pin
47. Stepney, spare wheel
48. *Rebecca*
49. For the smoke from the burning building to form a giant R in the sky
50. Article 50, Brexit
51. The chameleon and its ability to change colours

# SET 6

52. This is a multiplayer board game, published in 1995 in Germany, where players assume the roles of new entrants to a land, each attempting to build and develop holdings while trading and acquiring resources. The name of the place where they settle does not actually exist, though there is some evidence that a village by that name exists in Paraguay. The game is definitely not based on that village because Paraguay is a landlocked country and the game has water features. What is the name of this game that is sold in over 30 languages across the world, and is a staple at board game meet-ups?

53. What interesting, if alarming, event connects the following places: Ras Goh hills, Lop Nur, Semipalatinskin, Alamogordo and a certain city in Rajasthan?

54. The title of a 2001 Karan Johar film, *Kabhi Khushi Kabhie Gham*, pays a subtle tribute to an earlier one, which starred one of the lead actors of the 2001 film. What is the name of the older film and who is its director?

55. Born in 1844, Friedrich Nietzsche is a German philosopher, poet, composer, and Latin and Greek scholar who has influenced modern intellectual history and philosophy. In his 1883 book *Thus Spoke Zarathustra*, the protagonist has a goal for humanity. While the English translation used 'Beyond-Man' for this word, which is otherwise translated as 'superhuman', the German prefix used by him means 'over and above', and is nowadays used quite commonly. What is this prefix, a word that one would now come across when thinking about how to escape traffic?

56. Evangelista Torricelli was born in 1608 in Italy. He designed and built a number of telescopes and microscopes, which exist even today. His greatest invention, however, was an instrument in which a column of air is weighed against a column of mercury. What is measured by this instrument (a unit of which is named after him)?

57. The horns of animals such as cattle, antelope and giraffe have a bone core surrounded by a certain substance. However, a rhinoceros horn is made up entirely of a very different substance that is also found on human bodies. What is this substance?

58. Dr Joseph Ignace _____ proposed the use of a human execution device to the French National Assembly in 1789 to execute convicts more humanely. He hoped that this would ultimately lead to the abolition of the death penalty. His idea for a humane device was taken up by a certain Dr Antoine Louis who devised a machine

that would swiftly execute a person. This machine was sometimes called a 'Louisette'. However, this machine continued to be associated with the person who had first proposed the idea, even though he and his family tried to dissociate his name from it. This device came to be officially used for executions between 1792 and 1981, after which Dr ____'s optimism was finally rewarded and France abolished the death penalty. What was his last name and what was the name of the device?

59. The fifth Earl of Carnavorn was an avid Egyptologist of the twentieth century and financed the expedition that discovered the tomb of Tutankhamun. He was present at the opening of the tomb (but, contrary to rumour, was not killed by the curse!). In an interesting turn of events, in the twenty-first century, the interiors of the Earl's own estate became widely popular when it served as the setting of a very successful British TV show. What is the name of the Earl's castle and how is it better known by TV fans?

69. The French use this word to refer to a certain drink made using traditional methods from grapes grown and vinified in a specific region of France, which gives the drink its name. To protect this name, they included conditions on the usage of this term in the Treaty of Versailles, which was signed in 1919 to end the First World War. A certain country, however, while playing a major part in negotiating terms at the end of the war, refused to sign the treaty. Thus, they were not bound by its provisions. At the time of the signing of the Treaty of Versailles, this

country was going through a nationwide prohibition, so the French did not worry too much about this. However, as a result of not having ratified the treaty, once alcohol became legal again, domestic producers started using the French term indiscriminately for all drinks of a certain kind, much to the chagrin of the French. Finally in 2006, a new agreement was signed, which prohibited new producers from using the term as well as associated terms, while labels that had already been approved did not need to be changed. However, out of respect, many producers changed the label to 'sparkling wine'. What is this term and which country had this interesting issue with the French?

## ANSWERS

52. Settlers of Catan
53. These are all sites used by different countries for testing nuclear weapons. The final site is in Pokhran, India
54. *Kabhi Kabhie*, Yash Chopra
55. Uber
56. Pressure. This is a barometer and the 'torr' is a unit of pressure
57. Keratin. Human hair and nail are made up of keratin
58. Guillotin, the guillotine
59. Highclerc Castle, Downton Abbey
60. Champagne, the United States of America

Where?

# SET I

1. Forsyth Barr stadium was the first stadium in the world to grow grass in an indoor stadium, under a permanently closed roof. It achieved this by building the roof using ETFE, a transparent polymer known for its resistance to corrosion and developed for the space industry. This lets in light but blocks UV rays. Further, the interior of the stadium can be temperature-controlled and the eco-friendly irrigation system allows the grass to grow, nourished by the sunlight through the roof. Where is this incredibly modern stadium located?

2. In 1956, Dr B.R. Ambedkar led over 3,000 people in a movement to adopt Buddhism. He wished to do away with the casteist oppressions of Hinduism that he had been born into, and re-imagined Buddhism as a class and caste struggle. His version of Buddhism came to be called 'navayana' Buddhism. Where did Dr Ambedkar lead this historical movement?

3. This paste, called 'chapra', is made from a variety of red

ants whose bite is very painful, combined with tomato, onion, coriander, ginger, garlic and various other seasonings. The high levels of formic acid in the ants make this a very spicy dish. Where is this dish commonly eaten?

4. At present, this factory in New Delhi has carpentry, weaving (handloom and power loom), tailoring, chemicals, handmade papermaking, commercial art and bakery units. A very high level of cleanliness and hygiene is maintained in all manufacturing units. The administration also runs various vocational and technical training programmes for skill development, reformation and rehabilitation of people, in these units. A shoe-making unit was started in December 2009. The products manufactured in this factory are sold under the brand name of TJ's. Where would you find this factory?

5. 'Grung Tape', meaning 'City of Angels' is an abbreviation for the longest place name in the world (one word of 152 letters) and is the capital (and only) city of a popular tourist destination country. This name is a reduction by 5.92 per cent. We also know this city by another name, 'X', which means 'Village of Olives'. On the other side of the world from this city, is another city which also means 'City of Angels', whose full name has 69 letters, usually abbreviated to 'Y' with just 2 letters. That's a reduction by 2.9 per cent. What are X and Y?

6. John Cunningham captained squadron 604 during the Second World War. The squadron operated at night and

he earned the nickname 'cat's eyes Cunningham'. The British government encouraged a certain rumour about the reason behind his good eyesight, as they did not want to reveal that they were secretly using the newly developed Radar. The rumour was about a certain food that is naturally white in colour. A certain country bred them in their national colours and soon became the leading producers of this food, and their colour scheme became the standard. What was the rumour and which country is responsible for the colour of this food?

7.  Stretching across 2,300 kilometres and made by millions of beings, this gigantic structure is visible from outer space and has been photographed by astronauts aboard the International Space Station. What is this structure and where is it located?

8.  A certain popular household pet has two names because its original name was thought to be inappropriate during the First World War. What are the two names and where would you find the region from which the second name was taken?

9.  This coastal region of South India lies between the Eastern Ghats and the Coromandel Coast, in the modern Indian states of Tamil Nadu, south-eastern Karnataka and southern Andhra Pradesh. There are several theories about the origin of its name. It may have derived from the Sanskrit language, which when translated means, 'that which pleases the ear'. Which place is this?

## ANSWERS

1. Dunedin, New Zealand
2. Deekshabhoomi, Nagpur
3. Eastern India (primarily the Bastar regions)
4. Inside Tihar Jail
5. Thailand and LA
6. Carrots are good for the eyes; they got their orange colour because of the way the people of Netherlands bred them
7. Great Barrier Reef in Australia (the Great Wall of China is NOT visible from space)
8. German Shepherd, Alsatian from 'Alsace' in France
9. Karnatic

# SET 2

10. This is an award that is conferred 'in recognition of exceptional service/performance of the highest order', without distinction of race, occupation, position or sex. The award was originally limited to achievements in the arts, literature, science and public services, but was later expanded to include 'any field of human endeavour' in December 2011. The recommendations for this award are made every year, with a maximum of three nominees being awarded per year. Recipients receive a Sanad (certificate) and a peepal leaf-shaped medallion. However, there is no monetary grant associated with the award. Where would you be if you were being presented with this award?

11. X is a village in Malappuram district of Kerala which has been attracting the interest of various research organizations recently, because of a particular phenomenon that occurs five times more frequently than the national average. In October 2016, a joint team

of researchers from various institutions including the CSIR Centre for Cellular and Molecular Biology from Hyderabad, Kerala University of Fisheries and Ocean Studies (KUFOS) and universities from London and Germany visited the village to try and find out why this was happening. What phenomenon is this?

12. After the death of Charlemagne, the present-day territory of this country was called Lotharingia, which had a flag of two horizontal red stripes separated by a white stripe. The territory then passed into Spanish hands and yellow was added to the flag. 200 years later, when the Austrian emperor imposed the Austrian flag, another flag was made in protest, with a black horizontal stripe added instead of the white. On 26 August 1830, following a riot, this flag was hoisted above the city hall, and the following year, the stripes were changed from horizontal to vertical. Where would you find this national flag being displayed?

13. Only three countries in the world have not adopted the Metric System or International System of Units (SI) as their official system of weights and measures. The United States, Burma and 'X' are these three countries. 'X' is the only country in Africa with native Africans to have been founded by the people of the United States of America. The American Colonization Society founded 'X' in 1821 as a place for free African Americans to migrate to. More than 10,000 made the journey across the Atlantic, aided by the society, until 'X' declared independence in 1847. The country's name is a direct reference to the state of

these people. Which country is this?

14. Where would you find a millet beer called Tongba, served with a bamboo straw in a wooden container?

15. *The Lord of the Rings* is a famous series of books by J.R.R. Tolkien and in the 2000s, director Peter Jackson adapted them into a film trilogy. The films won multiple awards and are known in fantasy history as among the best-loved adaptations (though certain deviations from the book have been criticized). The films were shot in a certain location and part of that has been renamed Hobbiton. Where in the world would you find Hobbiton, with a replica of Bilbo Baggin's house?

16. The famous British conservationist Sir Peter Scott is widely respected for his various projects in the field of conservation, including helping set up the World Wildlife Fund. However, his various admirers have always been confused by his oft-stated belief in the existence of a certain animal that most scientists believe to be a fabrication. Indeed, along with American researcher Robert Rines, he even assigned a scientific name to this animal: Nessiterasrhombopteryx. However, a Scottish MP pointed out that this could be an anagram of 'Monster hoax by Sir Peter S'. Rines's response was that it could also be 'Yes, both pix are monsters, R' (admittedly, less catchy). Despite this possible hoax, Sir Peter does seem to have truly believed in the existence of this creature. Where would you find Nessiterasrhombopteryx (if it does really exist)?

17. Martin Bormann was one of Adolf Hitler's trusted aides and he devised various plans to ensure that Hitler's personal fortune was assured through various royalties. One of the means he devised was to declare that a certain representation of Hitler could be covered by royalties and that every time it was used, Hitler would earn a certain amount. Where would you have found these commonly used objects with representations of Hitler's face?

18. In *Game of Thrones*, Winterfell is the castle that is the seat of the House of Stark and proves hard to defend against enemies. Monty Python fans watching the show are likely, however, to look at the castle as a source of much amusement as it features in *Monty Python and the Holy Grail*. Where is the real-life castle that stars in two such diametrically opposite shows?

19. Christopher Columbus made four famous voyages to the New World. However, in none of these voyages did he actually land on the continent of North America! In the first voyage, he landed on an island in the North Caribbean, which he thought was Japan. He then set off southeast (away from the continent of North America) and landed on another island, which he named Hispaniola. From there on, through three other voyages, he ventured further south, always looking out for Cathay or China. He eventually landed on the continent of South America and explored it. However, he never managed to make it to the Pacific Ocean nor meet Vasco da Gama, as he had hoped to do. Where did he land first (the closest he ever came

to the North American continent) and where did he go to from there?

20. On the occasion of the International Day of Forests (March 21) Mr Sarbananda Sonowal launched the Sustainable Action for Climate Resilient Development (SaCReD) Initiative. This is to develop 'X', the world's largest river island, into the country's first carbon-neutral district. It is also planned to obtain World Heritage Status for this island in the Brahmaputra river system. What is 'X' and where would you find it?

## ANSWERS

10. Rashtrapati Bhavan, New Delhi
11. Occurrence of twins (Kodinhi is the name of the village)
12. Belgium
13. Liberia
14. Sikkim
15. New Zealand
16. Loch Ness, Scotland. This is the name of the fabled Loch Ness Monster, a.k.a. Nessie
17. On letters and parcels, these were postage stamps
18. Castle Doune in Scotland
19. Cuba and Haiti
20. Majuli, Assam

# SET 3

21. This high-rise building features in several popular Hollywood films and was called Nakatomi Plaza in the *Die Hard* films. It also features in the films *Speed* and *Fight Club*, among others. What famous real-life location is this?

22. In the 1600s, a rich Edinburgh goldsmith called George Heriot set up a school that would provide free education to fatherless bairns (children) of the city. Today, the school provides free high-quality education to the children of fatherless or motherless children. This school is located in the shadow of Edinburgh castle and most Edinburgh guidebooks claim that it inspired a famous fictional school that was the setting of a series of children's fantasy books and films. Where in the literary world would you find the school probably inspired by George Heriot's school?

23. In the iconic song 'Mere Sapnon ki Rani Kab Aayegi Tu' from the film *Aradhana*, Rajesh Khanna is shown

driving a jeep and Sharmila Tagore is in a train, reading a book. Keen viewers might have noticed that at no point do both of them appear together in the same frame. This was simply because Sharmila Tagore had to be away on certain dates, shooting for Satyajit Ray. While Rajesh Khanna shot on location in Darjeeling, where did Sharmila Tagore shoot her scenes in the toy train?

24. Rolex, a renowned manufacturer of timepieces based out of Zurich, is associated with several tennis tournaments and one of their best-known brand ambassadors is Swiss tennis maestro, Roger Federer. While they are known for a variety of clocks and watches, as of 2019, where in the world can you find the only digital Rolex clock?

25. In 1926, Rolex made what is considered to be the world's first waterproof and dustproof watch. The effectiveness of the waterproof mechanism was proven when an English sportsperson called Mercedes Gleitze wore the watch on a 10-hour swim. When the watch remained in perfect working condition after the swim, Rolex took out a full-page advertisement about the watch and its link with Mercedes Gleitze's achievement. Where did Mercedes Gleitze swim?

26. In 1953, a famous expedition was equipped with the Rolex Oyster Perpetuals, which continued working at great altitude and extreme temperatures. Where was this expedition headed and what historic first did the Rolex Oyster Perpetual witness?

27. In 1960, Lieutenant Don Walsh and Jacques Piccard

successfully helmed an expedition to the deepest known depression on earth's surface in a vessel known as the *Trieste*. A Rolex watch, specially designed for this purpose, was attached to the outside of the diving vessel. It descended a little over 10,000 feet and emerged in perfect working condition. What was this depression that this expedition had explored? (A 2012 expedition was only the second expedition to explore this region and once again carried a Rolex watch: the only known entity to have made this journey twice).

28. A famous author died in June 2017. In 1958, he had published a series of stories with the protagonist 'X' who went on to star in other books and is a much-beloved character today in books and films. The writer said that he was inspired to create 'X' based on his memories of evacuee children passing through Reading Station during the Second World War. The children had tags around their necks with their names and addresses on them, and clutched suitcases with their prized possessions inside. 'X', found by a family in a similar situation, is named after the place in which he is found, and today there is a large statue depicting 'X' at this site. Who is 'X' and, consequently, where in the UK would you find his statue?

29. Famed scientist Galileo Galilei was the professor of mathematics at the main university in this city. He wanted to demonstrate that two items, regardless of their mass, would fall at the same time. His experiment involved dropping two spheres of different masses from the top

floor of a very famous tower in his city. The unique (but unfortunate) feature of this building meant that he could drop the spheres without worrying about them hitting any obstacle on the way down. Though it is not known whether he actually carried out the experiment or not, the theory was tested and eventually proved right. The theory was further proven when, 430 years later, Prof. Richard Cox proved that in vacuum, a bowling ball and a feather fall at the same speed. Where did Galileo supposedly carry out this experiment?

30. Raja Sawai Jai Singh was an avid scholar of astronomy and established five observatories in Mathura, Jaipur, Varanasi, Delhi and Ujjain. The name, common to all five, roughly translates to 'instrument of measurement'. These were set up because the king had an extensive library comprising of books by scholars from across the world, but he believed that for a greater understanding of astronomy, one had to study the skies and stars oneself. The observatory at Jaipur is among the grandest and largest in scale. One of the instruments there is the largest timekeeping device of its time and is supposed to be accurate with a deviation of 2 seconds. What is this device and where is it found?

31. While a lot of people know that the first commercial train journey in India was made between Bombay (now Mumbai) and Thane in 1853, not as many people know that the first train journey in India was actually made in 1851! This train transported clay to farmers to build

irrigation canals. The clay was available in Piran Kaliyar and with the help of trains and engines that had arrived in India in 1851, it was transported 10 kilometres to its final destination, becoming the first recorded train journey in India. Where was this clay taken?

32. If you were standing at the confluence of a sea, a bay and an ocean, where in the world would you be?

33. If you were looking at a large diamond whose name translates to 'mountain of light', inside which building would you be standing?

34. In 2014, Kailash Satyarthi and Malala Yousufzai travelled to which city together to collect a joint honour?

35. Where would you be if you were looking at the original monument from which India's national emblem is taken?

36. Where in India would you be if you were witnessing an event called 'Beating of the Retreat' and on which date would you be witnessing this?

37. In 2019, a famous UNESCO heritage site built in the 1100s caught fire and was badly damaged. While this site is associated with the history of the city in which it is located, this monument has also suffered quite a bit, especially from the late 1700s onwards when it was badly damaged by looting during a revolution in the country. In 1831, an author wrote a book centred on the building and spent two chapters describing the building and its glory, and denouncing the state it had been reduced to. This galvanized the city into action and in the 1840s, they set about restoring it. Which famous monument is this?

38. With respect to the same monument as above, in the wake of this tragedy, it was found that some of the most detailed depictions of this monument, in 3D maps, exist in a very unusual source, which may just turn out to have some of the greatest renderings of world heritage sites. What is this unexpected source?

39. The Irula tribe are an ancient tribe from Tamil Nadu who are experts at catching snakes. A certain renowned centre of herpetology takes their help in extracting venom from venomous snakes for making anti-venom. What is the name of this centre and where is it?

40. Matsya (Vishnu) commanded Manu, believed to be the first man according to Hinduism, to build a massive ark to sail across the ocean in the worst of circumstances. Manu built the ship and sailed in it when the Great Flood occurred. He also carried with him the sapt rishis (Atri, Gautam, Jamadagni, Vashisht, Viswamitra, Kashyap, Bharadwaj) and was guided ashore by Matsya and Shesha. The place where Manu's ark rested finally came to be known as Manu-alaya. Manu-alaya has a temple dedicated to Manu. It literally means 'the abode of Manu.' What is Manu-alaya now known as?

41. The Svalbard Global Seed Vault (also known as the Doomsday Vault) is a secure seed bank on the Norwegian island of Spitsbergen near Longyearbyen in the remote Arctic Svalbard archipelago, about 1,300 kilometres from the North Pole. The vault was built to preserve a wide variety of plant seeds that are duplicate samples, or

'spare' copies, of seeds held in gene banks worldwide. The seed vault is an attempt to insure against the loss of seeds in other gene banks during large-scale regional or global crises. The scientists at an important gene bank in 'X', where new strains of drought- and heat-resistant wheat have been developed over time, were unable to continue their work in recent years and sought the help of the Doomsday Vault. The scientists have begun recovering a critical inventory of seeds and they are being planted at new facilities in Lebanon and Morocco. 'X' is a city in an ancient country that has been in the midst of a tragic civil war for the past decade. Where is this gene bank?

42. The Indian epics describe a region called Lavanasagara (salt ocean). The Ramayana mentions Lavanasagara in the episode when Rama goes to attack Lanka with the army of vanaras. Rama uses his agneyashtra-amogha in the direction of northwestern Bharat to dry up the sea named Drumakulya situated on the north of Lavanasagara. What is Drumakulya now known as?

43. During the Second World War, this repository held the original US Declaration of Independence and US Constitution. It also held the reserves of several European countries and several key documents from Western history; for example, it held the crown of St Stephen, part of the Hungarian crown jewels, given to American soldiers to prevent them from falling into Soviet hands. The repository also held one of the four known copies of

the Magna Carta, which had been sent to be displayed at the 1939 New York World Fair, and which, when war broke out, was kept in the US for the duration. Which repository is this that can be found in the higher levels of the video game, Temple Run?

44. In March 2014, a certain instruction was passed on to all male university students of a country, asking them to sport a specific hairstyle. The hairstyle is popularly known in that country as the 'Chinese smuggler haircut' because of its resemblance to erstwhile Chinese smugglers. In which country would you see this haircut and who ordered it?

45. For viewing purposes, the mirror reflects the light coming through the attached lens upwards at a 90° angle. It is then reflected twice by the pentaprism, rectifying it for the user's eye. During exposure, the mirror assembly swings upward, the aperture narrows (if stopped down, or set smaller than wide open), and a shutter opens, allowing the lens to project light onto the image sensor. A second shutter then covers the sensor, ending the exposure, and the mirror lowers while the shutter resets. Where would you see the iconic outcome of this cinematographic technique?

46. Peter I transformed the city of his birth into a major political, economic, cultural and scientific centre of its continent. The name of the city comes from a river that runs through it, whose name itself means 'a river'. This city boasts of the largest forest in an urban area within its borders. It is the northernmost megacity and in 2012

expanded to twice its size, becoming the largest city on the European continent by area. Where would you be if you were visiting this city?

47. This person first created history by setting a national record for the Greek swimming team at the age of 14. Quitting a PhD in psychology in the US, he turned his attention to music, playing in a rock band called Chameleon. He rose to fame because of a historic concert he performed in 1993 at an 1800-year-old theatre in Athens. This was the start of a string of concerts at heritage sites. Who is this unique artist and what is the name of the theatre where his iconic concert was held?

48. These iconic towers were inaugurated in 1999 and were designed based on the repetitive geometric patterns found in Islamic architecture, to exhibit the home country's culture and heritage. Each tower was built by a different constructor and one of the highest sky-bridges in the world connects the two. The towers get their name from Petroliam Nasional Berhad, an oil and gas company that occupies most of the building. If you were standing on the sky-bridge, where would you be?

49. This country was a kingdom founded by King Prithvi Narayan Shah. In the twentieth century, the kingdom was ruled by the Rana dynasty, who assisted the British during the first Indian War of Independence of 1857. Many people, especially those who had studied in Indian schools and colleges, expressed dissatisfaction and started a movement for democracy. After a failed start

on 16 December 1962, King Mahendra consequently established a new constitution where the country was governed by a 'partyless' system of panchayats. Which country is this, which finally became a democratic republic in 2007?

50. This World Heritage Site is the highest point in its country and can be seen for miles around. Its snow-capped cone is a well-known symbol and is frequently depicted in art and photographs. On 16 December 1707, it erupted and formed a new second crater and, though there were fears of an eruption following the 2011 earthquake, there has been no visible change. What is the name of this site and where is it found?

51. A tweet by a politician in this country indicated that a certain seat number was missing in its parliament. The seat between seat numbers 419 and 421 was numbered 419A. Which country's parliament is this and why would this seat not have been numbered, a cheeky little nod to the country's laws?

52. In which fictional universe would you be if you were on a flat world, carried through the universe on the back of four giant elephants who, in turn, were on the back of a giant turtle named the Great A'Tuin?

53. Beren and Luthien is a famous pair of lovers who fought against an evil force in a certain fictional universe. Where in real life would you find the graves of Beren and Luthien?

54. The Lincoln Cathedral in England was built in 1311 and at 525 feet, it was the tallest building in the world at that

time, and it stayed so for 238 years before a taller church was built in Germany. The structure that the Lincoln Cathedral surpassed, had held the record for a staggering 3,871 years. Initially 481 feet, it had gradually eroded to 456 feet. What structure is this that has been a wonder for thousands of years and where is it found even today?

55. The bacterium Thermus aquaticus was first discovered in extremely high temperatures in hot springs in the geyser area of a national park. Its incredible contribution to biotechnology has been the heat-resistant DNA polymerase that we obtain from it, which is an essential component of the Nobel Prize-winning process known as a polymerase chain reaction. In which national park were these amazing bacteria found?

56. When this 508-metre tall tower opened to visitors in 2004, it became the first to cross the half-kilometre mark. The building's design brings to mind a growing bamboo stalk, which culturally symbolizes eternal strength. It gets its name from the city it is in and the number of floors it has. Where would you be if you were visiting this tower?

57. The oldest known samples of a certain curved weapon or stick are known to be over 10,000 years old on this continent. However, this object also features in cave paintings from around 20,000 years ago! What is this object and where is the Bradshaw/Gwion Gwion rock art on which it is depicted?

58. Neuschwanstein Castle (New Swanstone Castle) is a nineteenth-century castle in Bavaria in south-west

Germany. It was commissioned in 1869 by King Ludwig II as a retreat in honour of German composer Richard Wagner. The castle has Romanesque shapes such as cuboids and semi-circular arches, Gothic shapes (upward-pointing lines, slim towers) and Byzantine architecture. This castle inspired an animator to build a castle in California in 1955. This second castle has attained an iconic status as the symbol of a powerful entertainment company. Where in the US would you be if you could see this version of the Neuschwanstein Castle?

59. The International Bank Note Society (IBNS) has a yearly poll to determine the 'IBNS Banknote of the Year', and has been doing so since 2004. Various countries have won this poll, but only one country has won it thrice and that too as a hat-trick, from 2011–2013. With exceptionally beautiful notes featuring flying birds, panthers, a map of the country and a monument in a rare vertical format instead of the usual horizontal format, the currencies that won were the ten thousand, five thousand and thousand. Where would you be if you were using these beautiful notes known as 'tenge'?

60. It is a well-known fact that Sir Arthur Conan Doyle based his character Sherlock Holmes on his professor Dr Joseph Bell, who had trained himself to be observant and identify differences in his patients' accents and gait to help him place them. He would also study their hands to try and deduce their professions (from marks, bruises, discolourations, etc.). Where did Sir Arthur Conan Doyle

meet this brilliant doctor who inspired one of the greatest literary creations of all times?

## ANSWERS

21. Fox Plaza, LA, California
22. In the *Harry Potter* books, this was supposed to have inspired Hogwarts
23. In a studio in Bombay
24. Centre Court, Wimbledon
25. Across the English Channel
26. Mount Everest, Tenzing Norgay and Edmund Hillary reaching the summit
27. The Challenger Deep in the Mariana Trench
28. Paddington bear, Paddington Station
29. The Leaning Tower of Pisa
30. A sundial, the Jantar Mantar
31. Roorkee
32. Kanyakumari
33. The Tower of London, the Kohinoor diamond
34. Oslo, to collect the Nobel Peace Prize
35. Sarnath (the Ashokan Pillar at Sarnath)
36. On Rajpath in New Delhi, 29 January (three days after Republic Day)
37. The Notre Dame Cathedral in Paris
38. The Assassin's Creed videogame
39, Crocodile Bank, Chennai

40. Manali

41. Aleppo in Syria

42. Thar Desert

43. Fort Knox

44. North Korea, Kim Jong-un

45. The opening scroll from the Star Wars films

46. Moscow

47. Yanni, live at the Acropolis

48. Petronas Towers, Malaysia

49. Nepal

50. Mt Fuji, Japan

51. Indian Parliament, Section 420 in the Indian Penal Code deals with cheating and dishonesty

52. Discworld, the universe created by Terry Pratchett

53. Wolvercote cemetery, Oxford. These are the graves of J.R.R. Tolkien and his wife Edith

54. The Great Pyramid of Giza in Egypt

55. Yellowstone National Park, USA

56. Taipei, the Taipei 101 Tower

57. Boomerang, Australia

58. Walt Disney World

59. Kazakhstan

60. Edinburgh. He was Dr Bell's student at the University of Edinburgh

**Who?**

# SET 1

1. This Indian-Hungarian artist was born in Hungary and educated in Budapest and Shimla. In 1934, at the age of 21, she moved back to India as she felt her true calling as an artist lay there. She combined an Indian style, inspired by the Ajanta cave sculptures, with European oil painting, and depicted Indian scenes, especially from rural India. She once declared, 'Europe belongs to Picasso, Matisse, Braque and many others. India belongs only to me.' This might seem vain, but she did have a unique style compared to her Indian contemporaries. While her newer Indian style was discouraged in the beginning, she ended up earning true success and won a gold medal at the Paris Grand Salon. She lectured in Lahore and was steadily ascending in her field when her life was tragically cut short by illness at the age of 28. Who is this artist who produced such beautiful works of art as 'The Bride's Toilet' and 'Hill Women'?

2. Gerald Rusgrove _____ and Charles ___ joined hands

in 1908 to establish their own publishing house after working together at Methuen & Co. The company was planned as a diversified publisher, publishing both fiction and nonfiction works. It was a profitable business. However, after the First World War, the company's fortunes declined because of intense competition from established bigger publishing houses. Gerald died and in 1930, Charles reshaped his company and made it into what it is known as today. Interestingly, they are one of the few publishing houses where the company's name is more famous than the actual titles. Who are these two gentlemen?

3. This polymath has the distinction of having two of his compositions chosen as national anthems of two different countries, and inspiring the national anthem of a third one. He was the first non-European to win the Nobel Prize in Literature and the university that he expanded using the money he won has prestigious alumni including both Nobel and Oscar laureates. He won the Nobel Prize in 1913 for a collection of 103 poems. The original collection had 157 poems but the poet, who translated his own work, did not translate all of them. Published under the name *Song Offerings*, it is part of the collection of UNESCO's Representative Works. Who is the poet and what was the original title of this work?

4. This Mexican salamander, called an Axolotl, is very pretty and unfortunately, very endangered! But it also has this

very fascinating condition, being the only amphibian that grows in size without metamorphosis. This means that it never ages or attains sexual maturity, but stays juvenile all its life. Zoologists call this the 'X' syndrome after a fictional character that has the same problem. Name this character.

5. Most people assume that these practitioners of a certain illegal profession wore a certain facial accessory to cover an injury sustained in battle, but in fact, this accessory was more likely to have been used to condition them to fight after sunset. Who were these people and why did they have this accessory?

6. Armalcolite is a titanium-rich mineral [(Mg,Fe2+)Ti2O5]. It was first discovered in 1969 and named after the three men who were closest to it at that time. The synthesis of Armalcolite requires low pressures, high temperatures and rapid quenching from about 1,000°C to the ambient temperature. Who are the three people it is named after?

7. This person loved sausages and stuffed pigeons. Unfortunately, he suffered from chronic flatulence for which his doctors recommended a strict diet. This led to a persistent rumour that is usually brought up to dismiss virtues associated with this dietary preference. What is the rumour and who is this about?

8. Treetops Hotel in Aberdare National Park in Kenya is built into the tops of the trees as a treehouse, offering the guests a close view of the local wildlife with complete safety. On 6 February 19___, something happened which

was recorded by Jim Corbett in the following way: 'For the first time in the history of the world, a young girl climbed into a tree one day a _____ and after having what she described as her most thrilling experience she climbed down from the tree next day a _____—God bless her.' Who is the person who climbed the tree?

9. *Metamorphoses*, a Latin mythological epic by Ovid, tells the story of a very talkative girl who is admired for her voice and how she falls in love with a man who rejects her. Eventually she is cursed to remain just a voice. The mortal man then looks into the river and falls in love with what he sees. Who are these two people?

10. They have broken the nose of the Sphinx, met Jesus Christ's parents, invented bull-fighting and mountain rappelling, brought a close to the Roman circus, discovered tea, started the practice of drug tests in the Olympics and met the Beatles. Who are these two people and where do they live?

## ANSWERS

1. Amrita Sher-Gil
2. Mills & Boon
3. Rabindranath Tagore
4. Peter Pan
5. Pirates and eye patches
6. Armstrong (Neil), Aldrin (Buzz) and Collins (Michael)

7. That Hitler was vegetarian
8. Queen Elizabeth II
9. Echo and Narcissus
10. Asterix and Obelix of Gaul

# SET 2

11. The 'X' is encased in a 157x98-inch box of triplex glass, a gift from the Japanese on the occasion of the painting's 1974 trip to Japan, the last time it left its museum. On 30 December 1956, a young Bolivian named Ugo Ungaza Villegas, stared morosely at the picture for a moment and then threw a rock at it, damaging a speck of pigment near the subject's left elbow. The painting has been a part of France's royal collection since the early sixteenth century. King Francis I purchased the painting from 'Y' after the artist accepted his invitation to live in France in 1517. What is 'X' and who is 'Y'?

12. 'X' had a novel way of avoiding restaurant bills. He frequently invited large groups of friends out for expensive lunches. When it was time to pay, 'X' would cheerfully write a cheque for the full amount. When he knew the waiter was looking, he would casually doodle on the back of the cheque, knowing that nobody in their right mind would ever encash a cheque with an original

sketch by 'X' on it. So the cheque would go unencashed, and 'X' would get away with not paying the bill. Yoko Ono requested a strand of hair from his moustache. In return, 'X' demanded $10,000. When Yoko coughed up, 'X' sent her a dried blade of grass instead, since he was worried she might use the hair for witchcraft. As a budding artist, he refused to be examined for the art history final of his degree, saying 'none of the professors of the school being competent to judge me, I retire.' In 1955, he arrived to deliver a speech in a Rolls-Royce full of cauliflowers, because he was fascinated by their shape. 'X' once delivered a lecture wearing a full deep-sea diving suit, which he refused to take off, almost suffocating as a result. He justified the exorbitant price of a painting by telling a rich customer that the paint had been mixed with the venom of a million wasps. (It hadn't been.) Who was this eccentric legend?

13. India's first dedicated space observatory, ASTROSAT, captured the rare phenomenon of a small six-billion-year-old star 'preying' on a bigger celestial body. These are binary systems in which the smaller star sucks material out of the bigger companion star. The small star becomes bigger, hotter and bluer, which gives it the appearance of being young, while the ageing companion burns out and collapses into a stellar remnant. Hence, the small star is called a _____ star. Which fictional character is this star named after and who is the most famous of these characters?

14. Ronald Reagan was the first divorced man to become president of the United States of America. Who became the first twice-divorced president of the United States of America?

15. This actress was the daughter of a triple Olympic gold medallist, the first rower to win three gold medals in the sport. Her brother was also a four-time Olympian and won a bronze in rowing. Her parents disapproved of her choice to become an actor but she was determined to work in this field and, with the help of her uncle who was a playwright, started out in this field and became a very successful stage and film actress. She made her Broadway debut at the age of 20. Despite having a very successful career (she won an Academy award for best actress for her role in the film *The Country Girl* in 1954) she gave up acting in films at the age of 26, when she married European royalty. After her marriage, she dedicated herself to charity work and her family until her death at the age of 52. Who is this much-loved actress and princess?

16. Hatley Castle in Canada has been used in films as the exterior of a certain famous school that brings together rare and talented individuals to train them to harness their powers productively in the world. It is run by a mentor, and his students or those he trains are collectively known by the first letter of his last name. Who is this individual and how do we collectively know this group?

17. This is a process named after a French scientist who first

discovered this method to stop bacteria from spoiling food. The process involves heating the item to 63°C, maintaining the temperature for 30 minutes or going up to 72°C for 15 seconds and then cooling it. Who is this process named after and on the cover of what everyday item will you find that word?

18. 'A powerful athletic body clutching a gleaming sword, with half of his head, that part which held the brains, completely sliced off.' This is a rather gory description of a particular item, by Frances Marion. The story goes that a librarian, Margaret Herrick, thought that the person described, resembled her uncle. Soon, the description became popular and was used to refer to this particular item. Who did Margaret think the item reminded her of?

19. This Roman emperor supposedly 'accidentally' started a fire to clear an area where he built his palace later, killed his mother and step-brother, used prisoners as candles by putting wax on them, crucified St Peter upside down and wrote love songs to young boys. He used to send his slaves to collect snow and ice from mountains and ended up creating ice cream. Who is this emperor whose name lives on in the world of computers to refer to burning information onto discs?

20. This person was known as 'the Wizard' for his superb ball control, having scored more than 400 goals during his international career. Since he used to practice a lot at night after his work hours, he invariably used to wait for the moon to come out so that the visibility on the field

improved. Hence, he was called 'X' by his fellow players, as his practice sessions at night invariably coincided with the coming out of the moon. On his birthday, the president of India gives away the Rajiv Gandhi Khel Ratna, Arjuna Award and Dronacharya Award. Who is this legendary player?

21. This explorer was originally a bee-keeper by profession. He led the first mechanized expedition to the South Pole and led other expeditions to remote corners of the earth. Later on in life, he became an active environmentalist and also devoted his energies to humanitarian efforts on behalf of the Nepalese people. He wrote an autobiography titled 'Nothing Venture, Nothing Win'. Who is this person who is better known for having reached the heights that no one else had with a friend?

22. This avid aviator was initially a French citizen. While living in France, he met French aviator Louis Blériot and a lifelong passion for flying was born. He obtained a commercial pilot's licence in 1929 and in 1932 carried mail from Karachi to the Juhu airfield, from where his friend Neville Vincent carried it on to other destinations, ending at Madras (now Chennai). The air mail company that this aviation enthusiast set up as part of his family company, eventually became the country's first domestic carrier, later becoming a nationalized entity. What was this airline and who is this pioneering pilot who set it up?

23. This Hungarian-born journalist moved from Budapest

to the US in 1846, during the American Civil War, as a recruit in the Union Army. After the war, he worked as a reporter for a German newspaper and then went on to enter politics. He co-founded the Liberal Republican Party but eventually joined the Democratic Party. He continued to work as a journalist till the end of his life, fighting corruption and carrying out ground-breaking investigative journalism. Today, one of the leading awards in the world for journalism, letters and music is awarded in his name. Who is this journalist whose name lives on over a 100 years after his death?

24. This iconic director used real arrows shot by expert archers from a short range, landing within centimetres of the hero's body. For the film *Ran*, an entire castle set was constructed on the slopes of Mt Fuji, only to be burned to the ground in a climactic scene. Other stories of his eccentricities include demands for a stream to be made to run in the opposite direction in order to get a better visual effect, and having the roof of a house removed, to be replaced later, because he thought the roof looked unattractive in a short sequence filmed from a train. Who is this legendary director whose work has inspired hundreds of others?

25. In 1850, during the California Gold Rush, a 17-year-old German-Jewish immigrant moved from NYC to San Francisco to sell dry goods to the miners. He tried to sell canvas to them for their tents but found they had little interest in them. So he made pants out of the material

instead. The miners loved the pants and though they weren't particularly comfortable at that time, they were the first ones durable enough to withstand the miners' rugged living conditions. The people nicknamed the pants after him—the creator of the product—and the name eventually stuck, becoming the name of the product. Who was this entrepreneur and what is the name of his multi-billion-dollar company?

26. This person was the first in his post, since the very first office-holder, to be re-elected after completing a full five-year term. In his long term he has, among other things, been Chief Economic Advisor, head of the Planning Commission and, from 1982–1985, the governor of the Reserve Bank of India. Eventually, he was elected to the post he is most famous for, which made him the only holder of this post to have had his signature printed on a currency note. Who is this multi-talented person and in which post did he serve twice?

27. This internationally famous actor and director grew up in poverty when his mother was hospitalized and he and his brother were sent to workhouses and residential schools. In 1913, he travelled to the US with a pantomime group and was spotted by a director who signed him up to appear in short comedy films. He was asked to create a funny character and came up with the costume that defined him forevermore: too-small coat, too-large pants, floppy shoes and a battered derby hat. Who was this actor, director and sometimes composer, who made some of

the funniest and most touching films of the twentieth century, and who had once been warned against re-entering the United States (for suspected Communist links) but received a 12-minute-long standing ovation when he finally returned in 1972 to collect an Academy Award for lifetime achievement?

28. Egypt's last independent pharaoh is one of the most brilliant and alluring figures of antiquity. A member of the Ptolemaic dynasty, the pharaoh was actually of Greek descent. The pharaoh's name comes from the Greek for 'glory of the father'. Who is this ancient character who has been immortalized in popular culture?

29. This famous writer, artist and filmmaker wrote and illustrated a science-fiction story in the 1960s and, based on his friend Arthur C. Clarke's suggestion, in 1967 he took the story to Hollywood and developed a script, though nothing came of it. In 1982, Clarke called his friend and pointed out many similarities between a newly released film and his original script, including the introduction of the lead character, a shot of their hands with an unusual number of fingers, and the special healing properties this character possessed. While Clarke's friend acknowledged the similarities between this and an earlier 1977 film, he could not sue the director who had made certain changes. It is widely reported that this director denied these charges and was later instrumental in awarding the writer-artist-filmmaker the one Oscar he won. Who was this pioneering artist and what is the name of the 1982 film?

30. This memorial is an iconic American monument located in Washington DC. It resembles a Greek temple and has a towering figure sitting in it. Popular legend has it that the figure forms the initials of his name in sign language. This is thought to have been done to pay tribute to the fact that the person was responsible for signing the legislation that allowed universities for the deaf to grant college degrees (the sculptor's son was hearing-impaired and hence he knew the importance of this). To whom is this memorial dedicated?

31. The tombstone of this French novelist is evocative of his works, which are futuristic, reaching across time. The tombstone shows a man emerging from the tomb and stretching his arms to the heavens. It represents a man whose imagination could not be buried with him. This novelist is known for his extremely popular *Voyages Extraordinaires* series and is also referred to as the Father of Science Fiction. Whose beautiful tombstone is this?

32. Sir Philip Pullman is an English novelist. Among his best-known works are a fantasy trilogy called *His Dark Materials*, published between 1997 and 2003. One of the protagonists of this trilogy grows up in an alternative version of a certain city, while the other runs away from home and ends up in yet another version of the same city. In 2003, Pullman wrote a short book that was a sequel centred on the city, titled *Lyra's* _____. What is the name of this city?

33. In 1631, Arjuman Banu passed away while giving birth to

her fourteenth child in Madhya Pradesh. Her devastated husband vowed to ensure that she would be remembered for ages and decided to build a mausoleum for her. It took 20 years to build and since completion, for the last 370 years, it has been considered one of the most beautiful architectural masterpieces ever constructed. How do we better know Arjuman Banu and her husband?

34. 'X' was born an Indian, staunchly opposed Partition and ultimately chose to work for the upliftment of the Pashtun people in north-west Pakistan. 'Y' was born an Albanian, but died an Indian citizen. 'Z' was not born in India and never became an Indian citizen. Who are these three Bharat Ratna awardees?

35. At a very young age, he burned down his father's barn. At 15, he blew up a telegraph station. At 16, while working in the railways, he forgot to set a danger signal, causing a derailment. He slept in his clothes because he felt that changing them or taking them off induced insomnia. He thought Wagner was Jewish, he believed that food poisons the intestines and insisted on starving. When asked whether he exercised, he said, 'I use my body just to carry my brain around.' Who is this supposed genius who was also a shrewd businessman?

36. Who was the first person to win two Nobel Prizes, and that too in two different fields?

37. This gentleman was appointed the first National Professor by the new government of independent India. He went on to become the first non-Caucasian individual to win

a Nobel Prize in science. A keen lover of music, he also investigated the harmonic nature of the sound of the tabla and mridangam. He started a company that manufactured potassium chlorate for the match industry. Who was this person who had a great fascination with light?

38. In December 1942, a certain event that dramatically altered human history took place on a squash court belonging to the University of Chicago. What was this event and who was the man in charge of it?

39. This lady was born in Madurai and moved to Adyar in Madras where she became a follower of Dr Annie Besant and the Theosophical Movement. After a chance encounter with acclaimed Russian ballerina Anna Pavlova, she dedicated her life to discovering and reviving traditional Indian dance forms and is strongly associated with Bharatanatyam. She and her husband invited Dr Maria Montessori to India, which led to the spread of the Montessori method of education in India. She turned down an offer to become the first woman president of India and focused on setting up the Animal Welfare Board of India. Who is this lady who spearheaded a cultural revolution?

40. As of 2019, the USA has had nine presidents who were not elected. They were vice presidents who were sworn into office following the death or resignation of the incumbent president. But there is only one person who assumed the roles of both president and vice president, without having been elected by the Electoral College.

Who is this person who is also the last vice president to have become US president from succession?

41. This gentleman made his debut on screen as a superhero in 1978. Audrey Hepburn had told him, 'You're going to be a big star,' and he was well on the way to becoming one, being especially associated with an iconic character. An unfortunate accident in 1995 left him paralyzed. Braving the struggle, he created a foundation to speed up research through funding, and to use grants to improve the quality of the lives of people with disabilities. Who is this real-life superhero who battled aliens and stopped bullets with his hands on the screen?

42. In 2018, a film was released that had been made based on a historic event in human history. The film was based on extensive research and interactions by James Hansen with the concerned person and their family. Various reports indicate that after arriving at their destination, this person spent 10 minutes alone near a crater and may have left something there, belonging to his daughter who had died some years ago. In the film, this is shown to be a bracelet belonging to her. Who was this pioneering individual and where was this bracelet supposed to have been dropped?

43. This man was the first recorded modern European to set foot on the continent of North America in 1497. He was an Italian explorer who had convinced a wealthy Welsh merchant in Bristol to invest in his expedition and had gained permission from King Henry VII of England.

He arrived on a land that he named Newfoundland (although people had occupied it for centuries before!) and it is widely thought that the name this entire region came to be known by was a tribute to this Welsh investor. It is also hypothesized that the flag of this country was inspired by the coat of arms of this merchant's family, instead of being associated with a much later figure in the country's history. Who was this Italian explorer and who was his Welsh investor?

44. This Oxford scholar and linguist was so fascinated by language that he created his own languages. However, being the passionate student of languages that he was, he wanted to give his languages a history, explaining how they had evolved and branched off into dialects. In order to do this, he created a universe in which different races spoke these languages, which evolved over the years and through use by offshoots of each race. Who was this painstaking creator and what universe had he thus created?

45. A 1922 play by Imtiaz Ali Taj and a classic film adaptation in 1960 (considered the most expensive film of its time) shot this character to fame. A Mughal-era tomb in Lahore is popularly believed to be her tomb, although most historians agree that she was a fictional character and some believe this tomb is that of Emperor Jehangir's wife, Sahib Jamal. They say that the name by which the tomb is popularly known is because of the pomegranate orchard around it and it has no connection to the character. Who

is this mysterious character whose tomb this is speculated to be?

46. This person became the first unmarried president of their country and also holds another notable first. The foreign policy adopted by their government has caused a rise in tensions with a country that shares part of their name, as they have made overtures to a superpower on the other side of the world. A lawyer by training, with a doctorate from the London School of Economics, who is this world leader and why are they unique in the history of their country?

47. The most translated individual author (103 languages) is also the world's bestselling fiction writer with an estimated 3 billion copies sold. The author also wrote the world's longest-running play (more than 25,000 performances). Who is this author of 66 detective novels?

48. This physicist and scientist played an integral role in making India a nuclear power. He was present at the first nuclear test as a representative of the DRDO and spearheaded the design and development team for the second test. He narrowly missed becoming a fighter pilot for the IAF but turned his attention to the skies as a project director for India's first Satellite Launch Vehicle. He even has a patent in his name for a coronary stent. Who is the person who went on to become immensely popular in his final official capacity?

49. The greatest tennis rivalry in the Open Era was between two women who played each other a record 80 times

in 15 years. They met in 14 Grand Slam finals and one thrived on grass and ruled the baseline while the other ruled on clay and mastered the art of serve-and-volley. They even teamed up and won a French Open and a Wimbledon doubles title. One was born an American and the other became one. Who are these two amazing athletes?

50. This famous writer was known for his short stories, novels and poems. He is also the first India-born winner of the Nobel Prize for Literature (also the youngest winner as of 2019). In 1910, he published a poem full of paternal advice and the lines 'If you can meet with Triumph and Disaster/and treat those two impostors just the same' adorn an entrance at Wimbledon and the club where the US Open is held. Who is this popular poet?

51. Felice Beato was an Italian-British photographer, one among a handful of photographers to document the aftermath of a watershed moment in Indian history. He also took a famous photograph of a person, almost certainly the first ever photograph of a Mughal emperor. What was the important event that Beato's photographs depicted (certain cases being recreated scenes) and who was his famous subject?

52. Hrishikesh Mukherjee, the director of the classic film *Anand*, is said to have approached this musician to compose the music for his film. If he had succeeded, it would have been an interesting poster as the film's title formed part of the name under which the musician

composed. However, the musician refused and Salil Chowdhary went on to compose some beautiful and memorable music for the film, and the musician also sang one of these songs. Who was this musician and what was the name under which they composed?

53. This gentleman was one of London's most iconic residents. He was not a great student who once wrote in his college notebook, 'Making pies on Sunday night... punching my sister... threatening my Father and Mother Smith to burn them and the house over them.' He went chasing after counterfeiters of the Royal Mint (which he ran), bribed crooks for information, threatened criminals and their families and then burned all his notes to cover his dirty tactics. Legend has it that when he served in parliament, the only time he spoke was to ask someone to close a window because it was chilly. Who was this eccentric genius who became famous for stating a theory in physics?

54. This gentleman was born of royal lineage in 1906. His father was from the royal family of Tripura while his mother was from the royal family of Manipur. In 1932, he began singing for the Calcutta radio station where he became famous for his performances of Bengali and Tripuri folk music, and light classical music. In addition to composing music, 'Karta' (as he was called in the music industry) has also lent his voice to 14 Hindi and 13 Bengali film songs. The father of one of India's most celebrated cricketers loved this composer so much that

he named his son after him. Which legendary composer is this?

55. This gentleman was the first US president to be born in a hospital. He had a bright future in the Navy but had to give up his military career to save the family peanut farm. In 1979, he helped end a war between Egypt and Israel. After his presidential term, he founded an organization that was responsible for the near-eradication of the guinea worm disease. He has a Nobel Peace Prize as well as two Grammy awards. Who is this charismatic politician who is the only United States Naval Academy graduate to have been elected to the White House?

56. This is an enzyme taken from the firefly and is used in biotechnology for visualization purposes. Unlike fluorescent proteins, these do not require an external light source. They use a protein that catalyses the oxygenation of itself using ATP and molecular oxygen to yield a highly unstable, singlet-excited compound that emits light upon relaxation to its ground state. It gets its name from the Latin word for 'light-bringer'. This term is also the name of an angel who was cursed to fall from Heaven in the Bible. Who was this angel and consequently what is the name of the self-lighting protein?

57. This teenager made waves in 2018, when she began skipping school every Friday in order to stand outside the Swedish parliament, holding up a sign that said 'School Strike for the Climate'. She is open about her diagnosis of Asperger's syndrome and Obsessive-Compulsive

behaviour and also adds that she has selective mutism, which means that she only talks when she wants to. She suffered from depression at the age of 11, which was partially related to learning about climate change a few years earlier. Since her protests outside the Swedish parliament, she has given a TedTalk and addressed UN representatives, and at a European parliament meeting in Strasbourg, upbraided the parliament for having convened three emergency Brexit-related sittings, but none on the dangers of climate change. Who is this inspirational teenager from Sweden?

58. Badruddin Khan Jamaluddin Kazi was a 27-year-old bus conductor in Mumbai's BEST buses who reportedly used to enliven his day and that of his passengers' by acting out entertaining scenes for them. He was spotted in action one day by a screenwriter and actor in Hindi films, who recommended him to actor-director Guru Dutt. Dutt cast him in one of his films and thus began a long and fruitful career for this talented actor, whose screen name was at odds with his teetotal real life! How do we better know Badruddin Khan Jamaluddin Kazi and who was the man who introduced him to the world of films?

59. This band from London was initially called The Detours and The High Numbers. They played a concert on 31 May 1976, which was so loud that a Guinness World Record was created. Eventually the Guinness World Record stopped listing this record as many people's hearing was being impacted by these concerts. The band released 11

albums over their five-decade career, which included two genre-defining rock operas. Which band is this, whose name was included in the question when perplexed parents asked their children what they were listening to?

60. This iconic gentleman passed away at the age of 93 after living a life filled with amazing history. His ancestry can be traced back to Charlemagne through his mother who was a countess. He worked with the Royal Air Force and did some secret work for the SAS, hunting down Nazi war criminals. During his tenure in Naples in 1944, he climbed Mt Vesuvius and three days later it erupted, just after he had left the city. His step-cousin Ian Fleming wrote a series of books about a British spy, and when they were made into films, this gentleman played one of the most iconic villains in the franchise. He met J.R.R. Tolkien and when his book was made into a series of films, he played an iconic villain in them too. He met Prince Yusupov and Grand Duke Dmitri Pavlovich, who were the royal assassins of the monk Rasputin, and then played Rasputin's role in a film. At the age of 87, he wrote and sang in a heavy metal album about his ancestor Charlemagne. Who was this iconic man who lived an epic life?

# ANSWERS

11. The Mona Lisa by Leonardo da Vinci

12. Salvador Dali

13. Vampire, Dracula

14. Donald Trump

15. Grace Kelly (Princess Grace of Monaco)

16. Charles Xavier, the X-Men

17. Louis Pasteur, milk

18. Uncle Oscar

19. Nero

20. Dhyan 'Chand'

21. Edmund Hillary

22. Tata Airlines (later Air India), JRD Tata

23. Joseph Pulitzer

24. Akira Kurosawa

25. Levi Strauss, Levi's

26. Manmohan Singh

27. Charlie Chaplin

28. Cleopatra

29. Satyajit Ray, E.T. (Ray's story was called 'An Alien Visits')

30. Abraham Lincoln

31. Jules Verne

32. Oxford

33. Mumtaz Mahal and Shah Jahan

34. Khan Abdul Gaffar Khan, Mother Teresa, Nelson Mandela

35. Thomas Alva Edison

36. Marie Curie

37. C.V. Raman

38. The first human-made self-sustaining nuclear chain reaction; Enrico Fermi

39. Rukmini Devi Arundale

40. Gerald Ford

41. Christopher Reeve

42. Neil Armstrong, the moon

43. Giovanno Cabotto (known as John Cabot) and Richard Amerike

44. J.R.R. Tolkien and Middle Earth

45. Anarkali (Urdu for 'pomegranate blossom')

46. Tsai Ing-Wen, the first woman leader of Taiwan

47. Agatha Christie

48. A.P.J. Abdul Kalam

49. Chris Evert, Martina Navratilova

50. Rudyard Kipling

51. The 1857 War of Indian Independence, Bahadur Shah Zafar

52. Lata Mangeshkar, Anandghan

53. Isaac Newton

54. Sachin Dev Burman

55. Jimmy Carter

56. Lucifer

57. Greta Thunberg

58. Johnny Walker, Balraj Sahni

59. The Who

60. Sir Christopher Lee

# ACKNOWLEDGEMENT

The authors would like to thank their parents and grandparents who have been pillars of support and channels of knowledge throughout their lives and always made knowledge of any sort seem fascinating and intriguing.

Berty would like to put on record his gratitude to the following people who inculcated and encouraged the spirit of quizzing in him—G.R. Diwaker, Ramesh 'Panza' Rajagopalan, R. Chaitanya, Siddarth Basu, Valekumar Krishnan, Sheik Ansar, 'Kabbalah' Ram Kumar and the authors/publishers of the GK books that stretch across several shelves of his library.

Akhila would like to thank her school, Besant Arundale Senior Secondary School, for encouraging her to participate in quizzes and having a well-stocked library, as well as her teachers, who would often slip fascinating trivia into their classes. In addition, she would like to thank the Landmark Quiz for strengthening her love of competitive quizzing; her many info-maniac friends and relatives and, finally, all the generous people who upload information to the internet and make knowledge so much more accessible today than ever before.